THE ALIEN'S FINDING

GRACE KENSINGTON

1

———

Consciousness came to Creia in layers. He felt himself lifting out of the darkness gradually, first aware of the cold air touching his skin and the presence of a soft humming sound somewhere near him. He fought to bring himself further, to remember what had happened to him and what had thrown him into the depth of the darkness and to convince his body to move. He could remember walking through the abandoned remnants of the lost Denynso compound, exploring the houses that had been left behind so suddenly it still felt like there were moments of life lingering there. In the back recesses of his mind he remembered hearing someone come into the house and turning to face them, only to be attacked.

Creia fought to remember something else. He reached for details, to bring anything else into his consciousness that would tell him what was happening to him. Feeling was slowly returning to his body and as it tingled along his fingers and through his blood, the image of the person who had attacked him gradually etched itself into place in his mind. He could see only the silhouette of a being. It was not as tall as him, but still taller than most of the other beings that he encountered, including the humans and the Mikana. The being wore a long, thick cloak that stretched to the floor and covered his hands. A hood came over his head and shadowed his face so that all Creia could see was a black recess. It was a terrifying image that made Creia feel like he wasn't looking at something that was living at all, but the breath and thought of death itself.

The memory of that image brought the panic in Creia's chest to a fevered pitch and he fought harder to bring himself back into his own body. Finally consciousness returned fully and he was aware of the feeling of a cold surface on his back, something beneath his feet propping him up at an angle so that it was as if he were lying down and standing up at the same time. He could feel something hard and tight around his wrists and around his neck, and when he strained against them they only tightened, pulling him back. Finally he was able to open his eyes. They ached as though they had been closed for far longer than he thought, and at first his vision was blurred so that he wasn't able to see where he was.

Creia blinked, squeezing his eyes shut as hard as he could and then opening them again. The action had helped to clear his vision, but he still couldn't tell where he was. The room was so dark he couldn't see anything beyond a few feet in front of him. He looked down at himself and saw that he was chained to a metal bed that was tilted, only the chains and a platform beneath his feet holding him in the near-standing position.

"Where am I?" he shouted into the darkness.

Though he felt like he had forced the words out as loudly as he could, they came through his tight, painful throat sounding hoarse and quiet. He drew in a breath and felt his lungs burn as they expanded. He forced himself to shout again, but only silence responded. He started feeling dizzy and his body trembled against the metal of the table that propped him up. Creia tried once more to scream out to anyone who may be nearby, but the words tumbled from his dry lips like powder and he felt the darkness descend on him again like a black cloud rolling up his body, stealing first his feeling and then his consciousness.

The next time that Creia awoke it was in one sudden, frightening moment. Rather than each little piece of himself coming back gradually, everything hit him at once so that he was suddenly aware of a hand on his forehead, shoving his head backwards and forcing it to tilt. Water rushed across his lips and down his neck, seeping back into his nose so that he choked and gasped. Gasping opened his mouth so that some of the water rushed inside and slid down his throat. Even with the painful choking, the wash of the water was soothing and he began to swallow eagerly.

When the flow of the water stopped, Creia opened his eyes and found himself staring up into the dark recess of the hooded cloak. He tried to reach forward to push away the cloak so that he could see who it was who was holding him there, but the chains on his wrists were still there, shackling him in place so that he could move only a matter of inches.

"Who are you?" he asked, the water having softened his mouth and throat enough that he could speak more loudly and confidently.

The cloaked figure didn't respond, but stepped away from the metal bed into the shadows that surrounded him. Criea dropped his head back to try to see where the hooded creature had gone, but he saw only a dim light hanging a few feet above him. He noticed movement on the edges of the illumination around him and realized that the creature had come behind him. A dark-gloved hand reached across the faint light and grabbed a device that hung beside it. Creia struggled as he saw the hand bringing the device closer to him, trying to fight it, but he couldn't get his head far enough away. The metal cuffs around his wrists cut into his skin as he thrashed against them, but the pain didn't matter to him.

"Who are you?" he demanded again. "What are you doing?"

The creature again didn't respond, but pulled the unknown device down closer and turned it so that Creia could see that it was a flattened screen and a set of diodes attached to long black cords. He brought the cords down on either side of Creia's head and pressed the diodes into place on his temples.

"Stop," he demanded. "Get those off of me. What are you doing?"

The creature didn't heed anything he said. He reached above Creia's head again and took the screen down so that it was in front of Creia's face. For several long moments the screen was completely black. In an instant, though, a bright image appeared on it, stinging Creia's eyes with the intensity of the light and forcing him to squint to filter it. When they grew accustomed to the glow, Creia slowly opened his eyes all the way again and looked at the image.

The screen showed what looked like a large, brightly lit room. The floor was a shiny white expanse flecked with grey and shimmering brushed metal tables sat along the center. He didn't recognize the space and couldn't figure out what he was supposed to be getting out of the image. The longer he stared at it, the more details he noticed. The far wall of the room was lined with white boards covered in indecipherable notes and shapes. Bottles and vials covered one end of one of the tables and another seemed to hold several boxes that glowed from the inside.

Creia noticed something in the far corner of the room, seemingly out of the bright lights of the rest of the room, and he narrowed his eyes at it, trying to make out what it was. It appeared to be a rounded tube that stretched from the floor to the ceiling. It had a faint blue glow that came from the bottom and in that glow Creia could see that there was something within the tube. Whatever it was inside the tube was chained around its wrists and neck like he was, but there was no table at his back to support it. Instead, there was an additional chain around the being's waist and another around its legs.

For a moment Creia was not sure that whatever was inside the tube was still alive. It hung from its chains as if it had no strength within it, its head forward and its arms pulled slightly up from its shoulders. The thought made a tremor of fear and disgust roll through him and he tried to look away. Turning his head, however, just meant that the screen went with him and as he watched, the thing moved slightly. As if in response to Creia's acknowledgement of his existence, the creature straightened just a small amount and lifted its head just enough so that it was above his shoulder height.

Creia wished that he could see more detail of the creature. He wanted to know what it was, and why it had been captured as he had. He didn't understand who could be interested in imprisoning him and what whoever it was could possibly think that he was going to get from him, or from the other creature that was dangling, seemingly only moments from death, in that strange room.

2

"Do you want to dance with me?" Jane asked.

Simran looked down at her and then back out over the rest of the group crowded into the bar as they celebrated the impending wedding. He looked back at her and saw a hint of a sparkle in her eyes.

"You do know what dancing is, don't you?" she asked.

He opened his mouth and closed it again, trying to come up with some kind of response, but then realized that there was nothing that he could say and shook his head.

"No," he admitted. "Not really."

"You don't dance on Uoria?" Jane asked.

"No. I've heard about dancing. The human women talked about it while they were on the compound and they even tried to teach a few of the warriors."

"How did that go?" Jane asked with the hint of a laugh in her voice.

"Not terribly well," Simran responded. "The Denynso warriors are made for power and fighting, not really so much for grace and smoothness."

Jane laughed and turned so that her back was to the

others and she faced him. She reached her hands toward him and smiled.

"It isn't hard," she told him. "Just come try."

"I don't know," he said.

He had done many things in his life that would have terrified others to their bones, but this was something that he didn't feel like he could face. The thought of being so close to her, even touching her, in front of others was something that he didn't want to contemplate.

"Come on," Jane said. "It's fun. Besides, just about everyone here is so drunk that they probably won't even notice that you are dancing, much less if you are doing it well or not." He hesitated and she gave him a slightly pouty look. "Please?"

He knew that he couldn't resist her. There wasn't anything that he wouldn't do for her, even if that meant risking certain humiliation not just with his completely out of control dance stylings, but with the arousal that was becoming increasingly obvious with every passing moment. Hopefully she was right and the rest of the party-goers had gone beyond the point of compromise when it came to their alcohol consumption and wouldn't really be paying attention to what was going on around them. He did take some comfort in knowing that even if the Denynso who were in attendance weren't able to consume enough that they would be impaired, if they did notice that he was experiencing the intense, unrelenting erection that came from being near his mate for the first time they wouldn't really care. He still wanted to be able to keep the reality of Jane private until he was able to tell her how he felt about her, but if a few of the warriors noticed, at least he wouldn't be completely humiliated.

Jane shook her hands slightly as if giving the gesture of

offering her hands more insistence and Simran reached forward to rest his hands in hers. She smiled and moved backwards a few steps toward the dance floor before turning around and taking just one of his hands to guide him the rest of the way. A few other couples were scattered around the floor and Simran noticed that he was not the first of the Denynso to be lured out onto the floor to attempt dancing. A couple of the other warriors were with their mates or other of the partygoers and attempting to follow the rhythm of the music that was thumping around them in whatever somewhat spastic ways they can think of. The image was reassuring and he let Jane pull him a little closer.

"Just move," she said. "It doesn't really matter how. You can just stand there and sway if you want to."

Simran laughed and started moving around in what felt like completely odd and nonsensical ways, but Jane nodded.

"There you go," she said, starting to move in ways that closely mimicked his own but that seemed a bit more controlled.

They kept going through the rest of the song and then into another. Simran saw her take a step toward him.

"Guess what?" she said.

"What?" he said, his movements faltering for a moment as he worried that she was going to tell him how ridiculous he looked.

"You're dancing."

Simran laughed and reached for her, taking her by her hips and pulling her up against him without thinking about what the motion would mean. Jane gasped as her body came into contact with his and she looked up at him with eyes filled with wonder. For a brief moment Simran tried to figure out a way that he could explain away the pressure of his erection that he knew she was feeling in her belly, but the words didn't come. Instead, he felt his eyes slumber and his body responding to hers even more strongly.

"Jane..." he started.

"Your skin is so warm," she murmured.

Simran nodded. They had stopped moving and he started again, swaying ever so slightly to the beat of the music. It was just enough so that he could feel her breasts moving against his chest and her hips brushing his. The feeling was pushing him closer and closer to the edge of his control and he took a breath to quiet the need surging through him.

"Only you can touch me right now," he said softly.

"What you do you mean?" she asked, not taking her eyes away from him.

"My skin only feels warm to you, but to any other woman that tried to touch me it would be so hot that it would burn her."

"Really?" Jane asked.

Simran nodded and dipped his head down slightly so that he could speak to her more easily without having to raise his voice enough that others might hear what he was going to say to her.

"You are the only woman in existence that could be this close to me right now, and you are the only one who I will ever want to be this close to me."

Jane glanced back toward where Ty was sitting on a stool by the bar with Samira in his lap and then back at Simran.

"Will you come back to my house with me and explain it?" she asked her voice softer now and filled with an emotion that sounded slightly nervous.

She was running her hands along his arms, watching their progression across his skin as if transfixed by this strange new ability that she had just learned that she had.

Simran nodded and she stepped back from him, taking his hand again and guiding him away from the dance floor and toward the exit. He didn't bother to let anyone know that they were leaving. He didn't care if anyone noticed they were missing or not. All that he could focus on in that moment was the need for her that was coursing through his body and the feeling of her hand in his.

3

———

They rode in silence through the city and out into one of the tightly packed neighborhoods that stretched out from it. Simran was amazed at how heavily populated the areas of Earth that he had seen were. It wasn't like Uoria where parts of the planet were open and barren, beautiful and strange in how untouched they were, and where the compounds where the species did live were made so that there were still sections where there are no buildings or interruptions to the natural layout of the land. It wasn't like that here. Instead it seemed that every foot of the planet had been touched and changed in some way. If there wasn't a home, a store, or a government building there, there was a paved road, a monument, or some other reminder that the humans had taken over the land completely and irreparably. It was at once fascinating and unnerving. Simran found the complexity and surrounding feeling interesting, but at the same time it was over-whelming to never feel like he was away from others. He couldn't imagine living in a place where he couldn't open his eyes without seeing someone else who was so close it was almost like they were using his very space.

Finally Jane pulled her car into the driveway of a small house and pressed a button above her to open the door to the small building in front of her. She drove directly into it and pressed the button again and Simran watched the door slide back into place. The engine quieted and Jane turned to him.

"Here we are," she said softly.

"This is your house?" he asked.

"Well," she said, "kind of. I live a couple hours away. This is my cousin's house, though, and he always lets me stay here when I'm visiting."

"He won't mind if we are here?" Simran asked.

He felt a slightly sick feeling settle in his stomach as he worried that the house not being hers would mean that they wouldn't have any privacy. Even if this wasn't the night when they were meant to complete their bond, he still wanted to be able to spend some time just with her. Jane shook her head.

"No," she reassured him. "He isn't here this week. It'll be just us."

They looked at each other for a few moments before she reached down and released the button on her seatbelt. Simran followed her lead and they both climbed out of the car, closing the doors behind them. Jane led him up a short flight of wooden steps and unlocked the door at the top. They stepped into the house and Simran looked around.

"Does this look anything like the houses on Uoria?" she asked.

"Not really," Simran said. "Similar, I guess, but not quite. We don't use electricity or have the appliances that you do."

"Really?" she asked. "I always thought that other planets were so much more technologically advanced than Earth."

She got a shocked, embarrassed look on her face and he heard her stumbling like she was trying to backtrack what she had said. He laughed and shook his head.

"It's fine," he said. "Uoria is very different from Earth. There are many different species and each kind of lives their own life. There isn't much cooperation or interaction. At least, there hasn't been until recently. The Denynso have an understanding of the technology and could use it if we wanted to, I suppose, but we have always lived this way and I guess we just don't see the point in changing it. We use the sun to fill batteries that power our lights and heat our water. We have luminescent plants for when the weather has been bad and there hasn't been enough sun to completely recharge the batteries. We use other fuels for our cooking and other tasks. It works for us."

Jane nodded.

"That's good," she said. She walked further into the house and Simran followed her. "Do you want to sit down?" she asked, gesturing to a large sofa in the middle of the living room.

"Sure."

They sat down together and Simran turned to her, ready to finally tell her what he had been feeling for her and what she meant to him. It was a conversation that he had never really thought his way through. Like the other warriors, he had always assumed that he was going to mate with a Denynso woman who would already understand the ways of their kind and have no questions about it. Now that he was faced with the reality that his intended mate was not one of the Denynso women but a human woman, he realized that he was going to have to explain the ways of his kind to her and simply hope that she was able to process and accept it. Though it was all he had ever known before the humans arrived, and not something that ever seemed odd to him, he was coming to realize that the mating traditions of the Denysno were not anything like those of other species, particularly the humans. Having to try to put words to the process and its meaning suddenly felt daunting, but he knew that he might as well just dive in and let it unfold in the way that it was going to. Her rejecting him would be the most painful and inescapable thing that he would ever experience in his life, but that was simply something that he was going to have to face. He wasn't going to know if she would accept him if he didn't give her the opportunity to. He drew in a breath.

"Jane," he started.

"Tell me how Samira and Ty met," Jane said, her voice overlapping with his.

They laughed.

"I'm sorry," Simran said. "What were you saying?"

"Um," she said, looking down at her lap, "I was just asking how Samira and Ty met. She just told me that she met him while she was on Uoria, but I didn't really understand the whole situation. Could you tell me?"

Simran nodded.

"She joined Zuri when she returned to Uoria after coming back to Earth briefly."

"Why did she come back? I thought that the exchange program was supposed to last for a few months for each of the participants."

"It is," Simran said, "but there was a special circumstance."

"What special circumstance?"

"She had only been on the planet for one day when she

was attacked by our greatest enemy." Jane gasped and Simran nodded again. "The reason that the Klimnu attacked her, however, is that she had run into the woods after hearing the man who was her intended mate was making fun of her because of her size."

"Her intended mate?" Jane asked.

Simran realized that he had unintentionally broached the very topic that he had wanted to discuss with her.

"Yes," he said. "Just like Ty is for Samira, Ero is Zuri's mate. Each Denynso warrior has one and only one intended mate. It is that person who he is waiting for from the moment that he is born and the person who, if she accepts him, he will remain devoted to throughout the rest of his life. She is his world and his meaning for being. She becomes the central focus of his life and every choice, every decision; every breath for the rest of his life will revolve around her."

"There's only one?" Jane asked.

"Yes," Simran replied. "In all the world, in all of creation, in all of existence, there is only one other person who can be the mate of each Denynso warrior."

"And if he doesn't find her?"

"He will live out his life alone, longing for her."

"And when he does?"

"It is one of the most important moments in his life."

"How will he know?"

"There are signs," he said.

"Tell me," she said.

"His skin will become intensely hot, especially when she is nearby. It will be so hot that no other woman will be able to get close to him, much less touch him."

"Like yours is right now," she said.

"Yes."

"What else?"

"His eyes will start changing color. They will shift from the color that they have been since he was born to bright orange."

"Look at me." Simran lifted his eyes so that he was looking directly into Jane's and heard her take in a breath. "Is there anything else?"

"Yes," Simran said. "He will need her. With every fiber of his being he will need to be with her. He will ache for her until he is able to be with her. Once he is, their bond is complete and nothing can separate them."

"Ache for her?" Jane asked.

Her voice was breathless now and when Simran focused in on her with his elevated senses he was able to hear her heartbeat pounding rapidly in her chest. She licked her lips and Simran trembled slightly. He couldn't hold himself back from her any longer. He slid closer to her on the couch and reached for her hand. Meeting her eyes with even more intensity, he brought her hand forward and pressed it to the swell of his erection. She gasped, but he didn't feel her pulling away. He let his hand fall away from hers and felt her stroke her hand along him cautiously, almost experimentally. An involuntary moan fell from his lips and he saw a hint of color cross her cheeks.

"Jane, I don't want you to feel like I am trying to..."

"I don't think that you are trying to do anything," she said, cutting him off. "I know what I am feeling for you, and if you are feeling anything even close to that, then I want to know why."

"I know why," he said.

"Tell me," she said. "I want to hear you say it."

"You are meant to be my mate, Jane. I have known since

the moment that I saw you and I have wanted to tell you every moment that we have spent together since then."

"Why didn't you tell me sooner?" she asked.

"I wanted a chance to get to know you better. I didn't want you to think that I was trying to force you into anything, or that I had just come here for this wedding with the intention of having fun with some random girl and then going home to my planet and going about my life without ever thinking about her again."

"I would never think that you could do that," she said. "I would never believe that you would be able to hurt someone that badly."

"You might be surprised at what the Denynso are capable of doing," he said.

She shook her head.

"No," she said. "I don't care what you do when you are in battle. I can look into your eyes and know that you would never pretend to care about someone if you didn't. I also know that I have never seen Samira as happy as she is now with Ty, and that she told me that she knew as soon as she met him that they were supposed to be together. She was feeling for him what I am feeling for you now."

Simran leaned forward and softly touched his lips to hers. It was a cautious kiss, purposely brief as to give her the opportunity to evaluate what she felt when he did it and then chose how she wanted to proceed. Even though she had expressed that she was having feelings for him, he didn't want to make any assumptions and press too far. He let his forehead rest against hers and they both took in a few slow breaths. Finally he felt her come forward and press her mouth to his again. He wrapped an arm around Jane's waist and drew her closer to him, coaxing her lips apart with the tip of his tongue so that he could deepen their kiss.

Their mouths explored each other for several seconds before he pulled away.

"I never told you how Samira and Ty met," he said.

"Do you really want to tell me now?" Jane asked.

Simran smiled and shook his head.

"No," he said.

"Good," she replied and caught his mouth again.

Jane's arms reached up to wrap around his neck and Simran swept her up and into his lap. Their kisses were deep and exploratory, but without any rush behind them. Each movement was careful and precise, enabling them to savor every moment that they were experiencing together. Suddenly this incredible woman was sharing his space and Simran not only didn't mind it, he didn't want it to end any time soon.

Their kiss parted again and Jane looked into his eyes.

"Would you like to come upstairs with me?" she asked.

Simran didn't reply, but scooped her up into his arms and started for the stairs that they had walked past on their way through the house. He rushed up them three at a time and when he got to the landing at the top she directed him where to go until he got to a partially open bedroom door. He pushed the door the rest of the way open with his foot and stepped inside the room. It was decorated in shades of white and blue, creating a feeling of peaceful calm.

Simran lowered Jane carefully to her feet and looked down at her with seriousness in his eyes.

"I need you to tell me that you understand what I told you," he said. "I need to know that you know what all of this means."

"I understand," she said.

"You understand that this is a life-changing and inalterable decision? Once you are my mate that will never change."

"I never want it to," she said. "I am not going into this lightly, Simran. I want to be with you. I have felt since the moment that we met that there was something about you so familiar. Maybe it wasn't that it was familiar, but that it was something in you reaching out to me. That part of you that has always been waiting for me spoke to a part of me that I didn't even know about; a part of me that somehow knew that there was something more for my life than what I thought. I know that this is a decision that will alter my life, but my life was changed the moment that I met you. I never want it to change back. I never want to be away from you."

Simran felt overcome with emotion. He had always known that the experience of finding his mate would be something powerful, but he never expected it to be like this. This was more than he could have ever anticipated, and more than he truly knew how to process. All he could do was let himself fall into the rush of emotion and need that was threatening to overwhelm him and let life change around him.

He dipped his head down and captured Jane's mouth. She willingly opened it to him, letting her tongue glide across his. They undressed each other slowly, allowing their fingers and lips to trace the skin that they exposed as each button opened and each garment fell away. Soon they were bare in front of one another and Simran traced her body with his eyes. She was the most beautiful thing that he had ever seen and he wanted to just stand for a moment and drink her in.

Jane looked away shyly and Simran lowered to his knees in front of her. He brought his mouth down to her belly and kissed it softly. The tip of his tongue slid along her skin and he moved his mouth up to her breast, taking it in and licking a tight circle around her nipple. She gasped, her fingers burying themselves in his hair and holding his head in place. Simran continued to lavish attention on that breast for a few more moments before moving over to the other to repeat his actions. When her nipples were taut with desire and he could see the flush of arousal across her chest, he moved his mouth down, kissing a path along her belly and occasionally stopping to blow a stream of cool air along her newly damp skin.

He finally made it to the valley between her hipbones and brushed his face along the soft curve of her belly there. His hands came to her hips to hold her still as he nipped his teeth playfully on her skin. The smell of her need for him rose up to him and Simran felt his body clench. He lowered his face down and dipped his tongue into the apex of her thighs, groaning as he gathered the taste of her into his mouth. He repeated the action, bringing his tongue further into her folds, and was rewarded with a gasping cry from Jane. Her hands dropped to his shoulders and he could feel her fingertips squeezing into his skin as he continued to explore her hot, wet core with his tongue.

After a few moments Jane's legs began to tremble and Simran took his mouth from her body, replacing his tongue with the pad of his thumb on the tight pearl he had coaxed forward with his patient attention. He circled his thumb slowly as he led her back toward the bed and then lifted her so that he could position her with her head rested on the pillows. She reached her arms up to him and he lowered himself over her, enveloping her body with his.

Using his legs to ease her knees apart, Simran stared down into Jane's eyes and finally allowed his hard, seeking cock to slip into her. They both moaned as he sank slowly within her and he had to bite his lip to maintain control as the feeling of her tight walls closed around his erection. She fit him tightly but perfectly and he settled completely within her until their bodies melded as one.

Simran rested his forehead to hers and remained still for a moment to give her body a chance to become accustomed to him. When he felt her relax just enough that he could move easily, he began to roll his hips. Jane writhed beneath him, her silky skin gliding across his and the scent of her raising around him so that he was completely surrounded by her. She lifted her leg and hooked it over his hip, granting him greater access to her and making each long stroke deeper and more intense. Soon he couldn't control himself any longer. Simran increased his pace and pushed harder, deeper into her until each thrust was greeted with a high, sharp cry and Jane's eyes closed as her back arched so that her breasts crushed into him.

Suddenly she screamed out and Simran felt her body squeeze tightly around him as her climax washed over her. The feeling of her pleasure pulsing around him overcame Simran and he felt himself spiral into oblivion, crashing into a series of strong pulses that met each of her spasms as he spilled into her. He felt the change come over them. The passionate feeling for her had increased indescribably and now instead of just knowing that he would feel the unbreak- able connection to her and absolute devotion to her safety and happiness, he felt it. She had fulfilled a place within him that had always been empty, and for the first time he felt truly complete. He had never realized that it had been there, but now that the emptiness within him was gone, he felt just how deep it had been.

Simran curled onto his side and pulled Jane in close to him so that he cradled her against him with no space between their bodies. He could feel her relax into him and her breaths gradually slow and deepen as she fell asleep in his arms.

SEVERAL HOURS later Simran woke to the cold feeling of Jane's body no longer being tucked against his. He sat up sharply, but found her sitting on the end of the bed, a large book sitting in her lap. He slid toward her and curled on his side so that his stomach touched her back and he could look around her at the book she was examining.

"Hi," she said.

"Hi," he said, kissing her arm. "What are you doing?"

"This was my great-grandfather's scrapbook. I looked at it all the time when I was a little girl. It's full of all kinds of pictures and documents and notes. He loved to keep things. He lived with my grandparents who watched me when my parents were working. When I was over there my great-grandfather would sit with me and we would go through all of the pages together. I was really young, but I can still remember him telling me stories about the things that he kept in here. When he died, my grandfather gave it to me."

"Why are you looking at it?" Simran asked.

"He seemed to have a story for just about every little thing that was in here. Even the tiniest ticket stub or piece of napkin or pressed flower had a tale attached to it that he would tell me in elaborate detail. There was a picture, though, that he would never talk about. He completely avoided it when we were going through the book together and the one time that I asked him about it, he just stared at it for a minute, touched it, and then told me that he didn't remember what it was or why it was even in the book."

"He never took it out, though?"

"No," she said, turning another page. "I always figured that that meant something, but he died before I was ever able to get him to tell me what it was or why he kept it in his scrapbook."

"So why are you looking for it now?" Simran asked.

"Do you remember when I told you that there was something about you that was so familiar but that I couldn't figure it out?" she asked.

"Yes," Simran said, "but then you said that you didn't think that it was actually that I reminded you of something that you couldn't figure out."

"I know, and I still believe that much of it is simply that we were supposed to be together, but that isn't it. It occurred to me when I woke up what I had been thinking about."

She flipped another couple of pages and then paused, resting her hand to one of the pages. She took a breath as if the memories of that book had filled her. Sliding her hand off of the page, she turned the book slightly so that he could see it clearly. Simran felt the breath catch in his throat as he looked down at it. The picture was yellowed with age and the clothing on the people in it told him that it was many decades old. It showed three men standing against a blank wall, and in the middle of them stood a far taller, broader figure with the long white hair and piercing eyes of a Denynso.

4

<hr>

"You have to listen to me, Mama," Maxim insisted, following his mother into the kitchen and watching as she looked around, struggling to find something to do that would distract her from the conversation.

"No, Maxim," she said, her voice tense with emotion. "I don't have to listen to you. We've had this conversation and I have told you more times that I care to think about that I don't want to talk about this. I didn't want to talk to you about it then, I don't want to talk to you about it now. I will never want to talk to you about it and I would thank you to show me the respect of accepting that and just leaving me alone.

"I can't just leave you alone about this," Maxim said, stepping up closer to her. "We found a secret passage off of one of Papa's rooms that had Grandfather's symbol on the wall."

"You know that your grandfather delighted in making those passageways. There are more of those throughout this kingdom than I think that anyone would ever be able to find."

"But this one led down to a room that had his symbol and Papa's. There was a hidden room that Kyven found accidentally." Maxim took a breath. He knew that his mother wasn't going to respond well to his continued story, but he couldn't stop now. He had to keep going. "It was full of weapons."

"Weapons?" Ellora asked, looking at Maxim with a softly startled expression in her eyes that told him that, if only for a moment, he had gotten through to her. Then she shook her head and waved her hand like she was trying to wave him away. "Your father died in battle. That was something that he and every other member of the Order knew was a possibility. It was their responsibility to take care of the kingdom, and that meant sometimes going to war. Of course that meant that they would have weapons. Don't you know that that is why the young members of the Order today are not allowed to be married or have families? It became too difficult to explain away their deaths."

"I know all of that," Maxim said. "Athan told me."

"You've been talking to Athan again."

It was said as a statement rather than a question and Maxim could see the painful blend of emotion in her eyes.

"Yes, Mama. He knows more about what happened to Papa than anyone else and I want to know."

"I know what happened to your father, Maxim."

"Do you?" he asked.

Ellora took a breath and looked away as if trying to gather the strength to continue with the conversation.

"When Athan came to the door that night, I already knew what he was going to tell me. I didn't want to believe it, but there was no other reason that he would be coming here. Before he left for that battle, your father promised me that everything was going to be fine and that he would come home to me just like he always did. There was something different about it that time, though. Usually when he left, he was incredibly serious and focused. The only thing that could break it was you two boys and saying goodbye to me. That time, though, he wasn't like that. There was a different feeling about him. It was almost like he was excited about something. He wasn't focused. He hadn't put himself into the mindset that he always said that he needed to when he was going to fight. It just didn't feel right. When I opened the door that night and I saw Athan, I felt like my heart had left my body. I knew then that your father was gone. His mind wasn't in the fight that day and they overcame him. That's all there is to it."

"Are you saying that it was his fault that he was killed in that battle?" Maxim asked.

"What?" Ellora asked.

She sounded hurt by the accusation, but Maxim didn't stop.

"You said that he was different before he left. That he didn't have his head in the battle like he always did and that it allowed the enemy to overcome him. Are you blaming him for his death?"

"That's not what I meant, Maxim. I can't keep talking about this."

She pushed past him and stalked back out of the kitchen, heading down the hallway toward her bedroom.

"He had Grandfather's sword with him."

Ellora stopped, but didn't turn around to face him.

"He did?" she asked.

"Yes. Athan told me. He carried that sword into battle just like he always did, but it disappeared the same way that he did. There was absolutely nothing of it left after the battle. You know as well as I do how strong that sword was. Grandfather forged it himself and there was nothing that could destroy it so completely that Athan wouldn't have been able to find at least part of it when he went back to look for Papa after the battle."

"Someone could have stolen it," she said.

"No, Ellora."

Maxim turned toward the sound of Athan's voice and saw him walking out of the front room of the house toward Ellora. She took a step back from him and Maxim could see emotion crackling between them.

"Athan, what are you doing here?"

"Your sons deserve to know what happened to their father, Ellora. And you deserve to know what happened to your husband."

"I know what happened to him. He died in that battle. Why dwell on it anymore? What good does it do to keep digging into it? You are doing nothing but hurt me and my sons."

"It's not knowing what happened that is hurting us," Kyven said, coming to Athan's side. "Maxim and I grew up wishing that we had a better idea as to what happened to our father. We didn't even have a body to bury and we never knew why. You said that it was different the night that Papa left for the battle and said goodbye to you. You're right. It was. Before each time that he left, he would tell us where he was going, why he was going, and when he was going to come back. Always."

"He didn't tell us that time," Maxim said. "He told us that he was leaving, but when we asked why, he just walked away."

"Some things just shouldn't be shared with children.

Maybe he finally realized that what he had been telling you boys was inappropriate and he didn't want to frighten you."

"You don't find it strange that he was so different to all of us that time? That the one time that he changed the way that he said goodbye to us was the time that he died?"

"Maxim, I don't know what your father was thinking the night that he left us to report to that battle. I don't know why he changed how he spoke to us or why he said any of the things that he did. Maybe he didn't actually change anything. Maybe he said different things and acted a different way each time that he left, but we are only remembering it seeming strange that time because he never came home."

"But you yourself said that he was always the same way. We were just little so it makes sense that we might not remember everything exactly the right way, but you weren't. You were an adult. You would remember what he said and how he said it when he left to serve with the Order, and you would remember why that particular night stood out."

"I don't want to talk about this anymore," Ellora said, sounding defeated. "That day in that battle those creatures didn't just kill your father. They killed me. The only reason that I have been able to keep going all of these years is because I had to be a mother for you and for Kyven. It distracted me enough that I was able to put most of that pain and emptiness in the back of my mind and pretend that it wasn't there. It never went away. I was just able to not feel all of it for a little while. Now that you are insisting on bringing all of this up again, and now I'm having to feel it all fresh. It is like he dies again every time that you try to talk to me about it. He's gone, Maxim. No matter what took him or why, he's gone. Talking about it and trying to get answers isn't going to bring him back. It won't fix anything. Why can't you just stop? Please, just stop."

"Listen to me, Ellora," Athan said. "I remember you. I remember you from long ago before any of this happened. I remember the sparkle in your eyes and the smoothness of your skin. I remember the way that you laughed and the light that came from your smile. When I knew you, I knew a woman who was stronger than most of the men I knew and more playful than the children. I also knew a woman whose heart was compassionate and open. You dreamed of a planet that was at peace, where everyone was united and no one had to be afraid. You wanted your children to grow up where they would be able to know the others that shared Uoria as their home and would have all of the opportunities that were available to them. What happened to that dream?"

"That dream was a ridiculous flight of fantasy from a young woman who didn't yet know what the world was really like."

"That dream was something that could have happened. Every time that you refuse to help us, though, you are making it so that it never will. You are making a planet that is already in torment worse, and ensuring that what your husband gave his life for will never come to be."

Ellora looked into the eyes of each of her sons and then looked back at Athan.

"It's gone, Athan. That dream and everything that I thought that I believed are gone. Please. I can't do this anymore. I can't keep living through this again and again."

"I'm sorry, Mama," Kyven said, "but we aren't going to stop."

"You might want to close your eyes and pretend that there isn't something more to this than what you see," Maxim added, "but we aren't going to."

"We are going to find out what happened and why, and we are going to figure out how to resolve it," Athan said. "Even if that means that we have to do it by ourselves."

Ellora shook her head and walked away from them, rushing the rest of the way down the hallway and slamming the door of her bedroom. Maxim could hear the sound of her sobs and remembered listening to her cry just like that for months after his father died. She wouldn't let her sons see the devastation that she was facing during the day, but at night when she went to bed and felt alone in the privacy and emptiness of her bedroom, she would pour out the emotion that she held within her, gasping out the tears until she finally fell asleep.

5

———

Feeling drained and defeated, Maxim followed Kyven and Athan out of the house and into the purple light of the setting sun. He missed Ivy more deeply at that moment than he could have imagined. He wanted to hold her, to lose himself in the sound of her heartbeat and the smell of her skin and to forget what was happening around him, if only for a brief moment. The lack of her presence was tangible, and so painful that it took his breath out of his lungs. In that way he felt he could commiserate with his mother more than he used to. He knew that Ivy was still somewhere in the kingdom, close enough to him that he could likely find her in a matter of minutes if he searched, and he still felt like he was barely existing. He couldn't even begin to imagine the level of pain that must come with his mother knowing that she would never speak to or hold her husband again. She could think of him and long for him, but she knew that he was completely out of her reach. The thought was overwhelming. He knew in that moment that he wouldn't be able to stay away from her.

He turned away from his brother and Athan to walk

toward the houses where he knew that the others of their travel group were staying. As if his longing had called out to her, Ivy was standing at the edge of the houses, her hands clasped in front of her. He stopped and stared at her. There was a moment when it felt as though time had slowed and they were being held in place. Finally it broke and she ran toward him, her arms held out. He swept her up into his arms, cradling her close and tucking his head into the curve of her neck and shoulder so that he could breathe in the scent of her.

"I'm sorry," she murmured against him.

"You have nothing to be sorry about," Maxim whispered back to her. "I understand what you are feeling. I know that you are just worried about me, and I can't tell you how much I love you. Not just for that, but for everything. Everything you are, everything that you have been for me. I love you."

"I love you, too. I love you for all that you have done for my life and all that you are doing to protect your family and your planet. I love you."

"I don't know what I'm doing or if it is going to accomplish anything, but as long as you are standing beside me, I know that I can keep going."

"I will always stand beside you. It tore my heart out to be away from you and I never want that to happen again. I don't care what I have to do or where I have to be. I will do whatever I need to do to be with you."

She pulled back away from the embrace and looked into his face.

"Were you just talking to your mother?"

Maxim nodded.

"I need to tell you about something."

He took her by her hand and guided her away from the

houses, not wanting to be close enough that someone might over hear them. Athan walked up beside him as he was telling Ivy everything that they had found in the bunker and about his grandfather's sword.

"Kyven has gone to get Emerie," he said, "I think that we need to go to my house and talk about this."

His eyes darted around them suspiciously and Maxim looked at him quizzically.

"Why did Kyven go get Emerie?" he asked.

"Just come with me," Athan said. "I'll explain when we are sure that we are alone."

They rushed across the kingdom to Athan's house and took the places that they had assumed more frequently in the last few days than Maxim could remember in his entire life. He reached over and held Ivy's hand in his, letting just the reality of her skin against his provide comfort and calm. Athan paced back and forth across the room until Kyven and Emerie finally came in. Emerie looked confused and frightened, but she settled down beside Kyven and turned her attention to Athan with an expression that held a complex blend of emotions that Maxim couldn't quite unravel.

"What is going on, Athan?" Maxim asked.

"I can't stop thinking about what your mother said."

"What did she say?" Emerie asked.

"She said that she knew that there was something different about that time that Aegeus left for battle, and that she knew that it wasn't like the other times."

"I don't understand," Kyven said.

"We said the same thing," Maxim said. "He was different when he said goodbye to us, too."

"That's the thing," Athan said. "He didn't talk to you the way that he did when he was going into battle. He always said the same things to you when he knew that he was going to fight. Why would he suddenly change what he said? What did he know about the enemy that we were going to fight that made him change how he looked at that battle?"

"And why did he have a bunker filled with weapons that he kept hidden, but didn't bring any of them with him?" Maxim asked.

"I don't know for sure about anything," Athan said, "but what I do know is that all of this has to do with the Klimnu. What we know about those creatures is limited. Maybe if we spoke to someone who knows more about them than we do we will be able to figure out what it was that Aegeus found out, and what he had planned."

"Are there any members of the Order who were around during that battle who are still alive and will talk to you?"

"No," Athan said, shaking his head. "Remember, Aegeus was extremely secretive about everything that he found out. The Order was highly divided over the issue of the Klimnu and no one wanted to talk about it. There wasn't even anyone then who I would have trusted to talk to about what was going on except your father."

"The Klimnu are gone. Who is left that we could possibly talk to?" Ivy asked.

Even as she finished asking the question, however, Maxim saw her eyes widen as realization settled in. She looked to him and he looked at Athan.

"Creia," he said.

Athan nodded.

"He has had interactions with the Mikana and the Klimnu for many years. He knows more of them than even I do, I would venture to say. Maybe he knows something that would help us to understand how the Klimnu fight."

"Any of the Denynso warriors could tell us that," Maxim

said. "I can probably tell you better than anyone that those warriors are fierce. They have fought the Klimnu extensively and they would know how they behave and how they operate in battle."

"But Creia knew them first," Ivy said. "One of the human women who came to live in the compound, Eliana, told us about being captured by the Klimnu. When she was imprisoned by them they told her how they used to be beautiful and happy," she said as she looked at Maxim and reached up to touch his face, the expression in her eyes telling him that she was thinking of the brief time of terror when they thought that he might be lost to the transformation of the Klimnu. "When they first started transforming, they went to Creia for help. By then he already knew that they were planning on taking over."

Athan stopped and turned to her.

"Say that again."

"By then he already knew that they were planning on taking over."

Athan let out a sound that was like a frustrated growl and curled his fists, slamming them on his thighs as he started pacing again.

"What is it, Athan?" Maxim asked.

"Don't you get it?" Athan asked. "Creia already knew that they were planning on taking over when they came to him for help because of their transformation. They had already started planning before they ever started transforming."

"We know that," Maxim said. "Mom said that after the conflict with the Covra, some of the clan never recovered. They wanted to exert power rather than ever letting anyone else exert power over them. That's when they left the kingdom."

"Exactly. All this time we've been thinking about the Klimnu, not the Mikana."

"What do you mean?"

"When the clan split, it was members of the Order who broke off and wanted to take over the planet. They weren't Klimnu yet. They didn't become Klimnu until after they had decided to split off. That means that it goes back further than I even expected. We shouldn't be thinking about the behaviors of the Klimnu. We should be thinking about the Mikana."

"What happened to the Klimnu after Creia denied his help for them?" Emerie asked.

"At first we didn't know. They were simply gone. Then we found out that they had left the planet and moved onto Ynn. It is brutal there. The climate is horrible and the ground is inhospitable. The ways of the Mikana, though, make it possible to survive and even thrive there. It wasn't until they found that they couldn't have the power that they wanted when they were on that planet that they decided to return to Uoria and try to take over again. That is when they were fully transformed. When we went into battle, though, they had just started. Not all of them were fully trans-formed. The more vicious they got, the faster they trans-formed. It wasn't the transformation that started them becoming greedy and cruel. They were already like that. It was being greedy and cruel that hastened their transforma-tion, and then the transformation made it worse. It became a cycle."

"Papa knew," Kyven said. "He knew what was happening."

"And how he was going to stop it," Maxim said.

"We have to get to Creia," Athan said. "We have to find out what he knows. We have to find out more about his interactions with the Mikana and what he remembers from when he was a child in the original compound. This can't just be about the Klimnu. Even you said that the division happened because of the Covra. They were allies to the Valdicians. When and why did that begin? What happened to the compound that made the Denynso divide?"

"If we leave in the morning it will be several days until we are able to get back to the Denynso compound to speak with Creia."

Athan paused again and looked at him.

"Not necessarily," he said.

"What do you mean?"

The older man looked nervous, unsure that he wanted to continue. He looked at each of the four sitting looking back at him and his face took on an expression of determination.

"Leave," he said. "Leave now and go back to your houses. Eat. Talk to the others. But pack your bags. Come back here at midnight and tell no one what we are planning."

"What's going on, Athan?" Kyven asked.

"Just do it," Athan said.

Without another word, they stood and left the house, heading back to the houses that they were sharing with the others of the travel group. The hours ticked by slowly and Maxim couldn't pull his thoughts away from the tone of Athan's voice when he told them to come back that night. Finally it was time to return and he and Ivy met Emerie and Kyven behind their mother's home. They all exchanged glances that held questions along with their resignation to whatever was happening.

By the time they made it back to Athan's house, he was standing outside, two large bags over his shoulder.

"Did anyone follow you?" he asked.

"No," Maxim replied.

"And you told no one that we were leaving?"

"No one," Maxim confirmed.

"Come on. Move quickly. We can't risk the guards finding us."

They moved along quickly behind Athan as he walked in long strides across the kingdom toward the gate that Maxim and Ivy had used the first time that they visited. There should have been a guard standing there, but the entire area stood silent and empty.

"Athan, are you supposed to be on guard duty tonight?" he asked.

"Yes," Athan said back to him over his shoulder, keeping his voice just loud enough for Maxim to hear. "It is the only reason that we were able to do this tonight."

"Won't you be in serious trouble with the Order if they find out that you aren't in your post?"

"What I have already told you has already put me in serious danger. What I plan to show you tonight would have me killed if any of the Order was to find out. I have come this far. I might as well see it through."

They continued on through the gate and out of the kingdom. Rather than venturing out across the open space in front of the kingdom, however, he remained close to the wall, following it with one hand outstretched as if he was searching for something. Maxim's mind immediately went to the stones that Athan touched to open the Order tunnels that wound beneath the kingdom. They had followed the curve of the wall until they were nearly at the back of the kingdom when Athan finally stopped. He stepped closer to the wall and ran his fingertips across it again.

"Do you need light?" Maxim asked.

"No," Athan said. "I don't want to call any attention to us."

He continued to feel along the wall, and then Maxim heard a click. The ground beneath his feet trembled slightly and then the moonlight illuminated the grass in front of them just enough that Maxim saw a section slide open. It was much like the tunnel, except that it didn't seem the ground was creating a ramp. Rather, it was opening and a moment later the shape of something dark rose up out of the grass. Ivy gasped and Maxim reached for her, taking her by the hand and pulling her back behind him protectively. He didn't know what was happening, but a sense of intrigue flowed through him.

The shape rose only a few feet and then stopped. Athan stepped forward; paused briefly, and then walked up to what Maxim now realized was a small metal building. Athan reached into his pocket and withdrew a small piece of intricately shaped metal. He pressed it into a recessed section of the wall and the outline of it lit up in a bright blue glow. A moment later an area of the wall slid down and then inward, folding as it went to create a set of steps leading down.

"Follow me," Athan said.

They all moved forward, Maxim approaching the doorway first with Ivy close behind him. Though the building had only risen out of the ground a few feet, the metal steps that had formed led far enough down that Maxim only needed to duck his head for the first few steps. He moved down the stairs as quickly as he could to allow the others to get into the cover and protection of the building. As soon as Kyven's feet touched the floor, Athan touched a panel on the wall beside him and the steps folded themselves back up to create a solid wall in the building again. There was a low groaning sound and the building itself began to move, lowering back down. Though he knew that they were deep enough beneath the ground that the building frame wouldn't come close to them, it was still a strange sensation to watch the space around himself progressively shrinking and Maxim fought the urge to crouch down.

Finally the metal frame locked into place and Athan urged them to continue. They followed him down a hallway that illuminated in the same progressive color pattern that the tunnel did, and Maxim found himself watching ahead of them out of nervousness that he would see the ceiling brighten as someone approached. The panels remained dark, however, until they crossed under them and soon they exited the hallway into another room. There were several large forms hunkering in the center of the room covered with large cloths. Athan approached one of them with a nostalgic, reverent look on his face and flattened his hands to it.

"They're still here," he whispered almost to himself. "I was hoping that they would be."

"What are they?" Maxim asked.

"I know that you probably don't remember it, but there was a time when moving around the planet and even leaving the planet for brief visits to others was not completely out of the norm for the Mikana. We had some of the most advanced technology in the galaxy. That all changed, though, and the Klimnu were the last to leave and return. It has been many decades since we've utilized any of the technology that we developed for fast and reliable transportation. The kingdom leaders thought it was too dangerous to have transportation that allowed the people of the kingdom to move about as they pleased. They banned the use of the technology and destroyed all of the vehicles." He gazed down at the form beneath his hands. "Most of them. The Order preserved these, kept them aside out of the destruction pits to ensure that they were available in the event of an emergency." He gave a mirthless laugh. "I suppose that their idea of what may be an emergency is somewhat different than ours."

He stopped talking and grabbed onto the cloth, yanking it away to reveal a black vehicle that sat on the floor without wheels. It was unlike anything that Maxim remembered. If he dug deeply into his memories he thought that he might remember a few instances of his father talking about the use of transportation technology, but his lucid memories were all of everyone walking everywhere. He couldn't remember ever seeing, much less riding in, something like this.

"Do they still work?" Kyven asked.

Athan glanced at him and then back at the vehicle.

"I can't imagine why not. They were designed for absolute reliability. Their fuel cores could last more than a century before needing recharging.

"How do we use them?" Maxim asked.

His voice sounded strong and determined, and Athan turned to him with the hint of an approving smile on his face. He moved over to the next form and pulled away the cloth.

"Get in," he said. "Kyven, ride with me."

Maxim approached the vehicle and saw that the center was a deep well molded into seats. He helped Ivy in and then climbed inside, settling into the seat positioned in front of a bank of control panels. His heart started pounding and he was unsure of what he needed to do.

"Do you want me to do it?" Ivy asked from beside him.

He glanced over at her.

"I drive on Earth. Do you want me to try to pilot it?"

There was nothing judgmental or teasing in the question and Maxim touched her cheek gently.

"Yes," he said.

They switched places and Ivy settled into the control seat while he sat beside her. It felt both strange and liberating to hand over the control of the vehicle to her. He was accustomed to wanting to be strong and do everything himself, even when following the commands of the king. Ivy had offered herself to him as his partner, however, and that meant that he could lean on her when he needed her. Driving was a skill that she had that he didn't, and even though he assumed that these Mikana vehicles were very different than the ones on Earth, this was her way of offering her help, being there for him, and making sure that he was safe and had what he needed to do what they had to do. It was all that he had asked of her and he finally felt like they were truly coming together.

"Are you ready?" Athan called to them.

"Yes," Ivy called back.

"Do you have your restraints on?"

Maxim and Ivy adjusted their restraints and ensured that they were firmly in place.

"Yes," she called back again.

"Press the blue button in front of you and sit very still."

Ivy complied and they both sat still as a clear, bubble-like top slid into place over them. Despite its age, the material was still crystalline and he was able to see around him almost as though there was nothing there.

"Ivy?"

Athan's voice came at them from in front of Ivy and Maxim jumped.

"Athan?" he said.

"This is the inter-craft communication system. As long as your top is up you are fully protected, but you will not be able to hear me calling to you. If you have something that you need to say to me, just press the purple button in front of you and it will connect directly to my ship. It will work anywhere on Uoria no matter how far we are apart. Hopefully there won't be a time when we are out of each other's sight, though. Are you ready to go?"

"I am."

"Good. Touch your hands to the screen in front of you. It will measure size and shape so that it can customize the control bar for you. That way it will be as responsive as possible while minimizing discomfort and error. There is a way that you can tell the craft to pilot itself, but that requires you to know exactly where you are going and it does not account for sudden changes in your travel. It's best to just go ahead and pilot it yourself unless we are moving through large open places that don't really require us to make decisions."

"Alright," Ivy said.

Maxim watched her press her hands to the screen and a series of multicolored lights appeared beneath them. The screen scanned her hands in several directions and then made a low beeping sound. Ivy pulled her hands away and there was a faint glowing outline of them on the screen for several seconds before it disappeared and a curved black bar came out of the control panel toward her.

"I have my control bar," she said to Athan.

"Good. I'm going to go first. When I am in front of you and have gone a few feet, press the green button, take your control bar and we'll go. Follow me as closely as you can without bumping me, and do as I do. I'm going to have to trust you on this."

"I will, Athan."

"Here we go."

(TO BE CONTINUED IN BOOK VIII...)

"That's a Denynso," Simran said, sitting up and swinging his legs around so that they hung off of the end of the bed like Jane's. "At least, that's what it looks like."

"I thought so, too," she said, allowing him to pull the book off of her lap and into his so that he could look more closely at the picture.

"There are a few things that are little different about him," Simran said, "but it is unmistakable. The size, the hair, the eyes. I don't know what else it could be."

"It doesn't make any sense, though," Jane said. "This picture is extremely old. The Denynso and Earth didn't have any interaction when it was taken. I don't understand how it could possibly be a Denynso with human men."

"I don't, either," Simran said. "I can't help but think that it means something, though. The only thing that I can think of to do is bring it to show Pyra and Eden. Pyra is the leader of the Denynso warriors. Other than Creia, our king, he is the most knowledgeable and honored of us." He said the words with as much confidence as he could, trying to force his mind away from the horrors that had occurred on the Nyx 23 settlement at the hands of this leader. Pyra had acknowledged his wrong doing and asked for their forgiveness. Though he struggled like many of the others, Simran knew that he had to let go. "His mate, Eden, was the first human woman to come to the compound and end up staying with us. She has actually become Denynso."

"What?" Jane asked.

"Eden was a human woman but now she is Denynso."

"How did that happen? Does that happen to all human women who mate with Denynso warriors?"

There was a faint look of fear on her face and Simran felt his stomach sink slightly.

"The thought of that terrifies you, doesn't it?" he asked. "You weren't really prepared for the realities of being my mate."

"That's not it," Jane insisted. "I just don't know these things. You need to be patient with me. This was not something that I expected to happen in my life and I feel like I am navigating it by the minute."

Simran wrapped an arm around her waist and pulled her in for a kiss.

"So do I," he said. "Don't worry. I am right here with you. We're going to figure it out together." Jane laughed softly and he gave her a smile. "No," he told her, "most human women do not automatically turn into Denynso women when they mate with a Denynso man. Though Pyra was the first of our clan to mate with a human woman, there have been plenty others after, as you know, and they are all still perfectly human. No signs of altering DNA yet."

Jane smile and kissed him again.

"Then what happened?" she asked.

"When she was first in the compound, she was tricked by

a Klimnu. They were the greatest enemies of our kind and some of them had the ability to mimic the appearance of others. That particular creature took on the appearance of Pyra so that Eden would trust it and then attacked her. It nearly killed her, but the real Pyra found her in just enough time that he was able to get her to our healer, Ciyrs, and he saved her life. The healing that she needed was extensive, however, and in the process she was changed. We still don't know how it happened, or why, but she now has the DNA of a Denynso and has started exhibiting some of the characteristics of a Denynso woman. She hasn't grown any, though, so she is still quite small compared to the other women of the clan."

"And you think that showing them the picture will help?" she asked.

"Yes," he told her.

"Alright. Let's get dressed and we'll go find them."

AFTER A LONG SHOWER they got dressed and headed out. Simran directed Jane to the house where they were staying and carried the scrapbook inside. He found Pyra sitting in the kitchen sipping a drink called coffee that they had never had on the Denynso compound but of which Pyra had become quite fond of in their time on Earth. The warrior leader glanced over at them and swallowed hard, setting his mug down on the table.

"What happened to you last night?" he asked.

"What do you mean?" Simran asked, trying to look like he didn't know what Pyra was talking about.

"We went looking for you when the party wound down, but you weren't at the bar anymore. Someone said that they saw you leaving with Jane."

Jane stepped out from behind Simran and Simran wrapped an arm around her.

"I did leave with Jane," he said with a smile.

"Congratulations!" Pyra said loudly, getting up to shake Simran's hand.

"Thanks," Simran said, "but that's not what we're here to talk about. Is Eden around?"

"Yeah. She's upstairs with the baby. Is everything alright?"

"We're not sure. We just need to talk to both of you."

"Come on up."

Pyra led them up the stairs to a bedroom. Eden was sitting in a rocking chair cradling Lysander in her arms and singing quietly to him.

"I'm sorry," Simran said, "We didn't mean to intrude."

"No," Eden said with a wide smile, "it's fine. Come in."

They stepped inside and Simran looked at them both.

"Jane has been telling me that I was really familiar to her, that I reminded her of something, but she didn't know what. It wasn't until this morning that she figured it out." He showed them the scrapbook. "This belonged to her great-grandfather. It's full of every kind of memento imaginable and she said that he used to tell her stories about everything that was in it. Everything except for this one particular picture. That picture he wouldn't talk about and would even act like he had no idea what it was or why it was in the scrapbook."

"Is it OK if we look at the picture, Jane?" Eden asked.

"That's fine," Jane said. "That's why we came here. Simran thinks that it is significant but we don't know why. You and Pyra might be able to help us."

Simran lowered the scrapbook to the bed and flipped through the pages until he got to the picture. Just looking at it again sent new chills down his spine and he spun the book toward Pyra as quickly as he could. He gestured toward the picture and Pyra leaned down to look at it. Simran saw his eyes narrow and his massive hands come to the side of the book so that he could look more closely at it.

"Is that..." he started.

He brought the book over to Eden and held it so that she could look at the picture.

"A Denynso," she said, finishing his thought with her own surprised exclamation.

"That's what we thought, too," Simran said.

He saw Eden squint at the picture much like he had and she shook her head.

"I've seen this before," she said.

"You have?" Jane asked, sounding stunned.

"Yes," Eden said. "Not in this book, though. I've seen it somewhere else."

"Where?" Pyra asked.

Eden shook her head again.

"I can't put my finger on it. I know that I have though." She shuddered slightly and looked down at Lysander's face, looking as much like she just wanted to gaze at her son as she did like she didn't want to look at the picture any longer. "Something about it bothers me. I don't remember where or why I've seen it, but I know that it isn't a good thing that I have."

Pyra pulled the book back in front of him again and looked back down at the picture.

"There's something strange about the Denynso in this picture, if that's what he is, of course."

"I don't see what else he could be," Eden said. "He has all of the characteristics."

"Yeah, but there's some things about him that are a little

off. I can't really explain exactly what it is, but he just looks different."

"He's smaller," Jane offered. "Now that I've seen you in person I really notice it, but that Denynso is not as big in comparison to the men beside him as you would be if you were standing next to them. Could he be very young?"

"No," Simran said. "Look at his hair. You can tell what stage of life a Denynso is in by his hair. This is a grown adult. He is at full height."

"His face looks a little different, too," Eden offered. "I'm not exactly sure why, but it doesn't look like a Denynso face."

"Do you know when this picture was taken?" Pyra asked.

"No," Jane admitted. "I don't know anything about it. I mean, I know that it isn't a contemporary picture. It has looked old and worn ever since I was a little girl. And look at the clothing. It is definitely an old picture."

"Is there anything written on the back?" Eden asked.

"Written on the back?" Pyra asked.

"Yes," Eden said. "Remember how Lynx found out Rain's name because he saw it written on the back of a picture of her? That is something that people used to do here. If you put a picture in a scrapbook or a frame, you wrote who it was and when it was taken on the back so that you could remember later when you look at it."

"I don't know," Jane said. "I've only ever seen it in the book. My great-grandfather never checked, not even when I asked him about the picture."

"Would it be OK with you if we took it out?" Simran asked. "I'm sure that we can get it back in."

Jane nodded.

"Of course," she said. "It's about time I find out the real story behind that picture anyway."

Pyra put the book carefully on the bed and grasped the

corner of the picture. Holding the rest of the book down with his other hand, he gently started to peel the picture up and off of the page. It came more easily than Simran would have suspected, which only further confirmed to him the age of the picture. Pyra handed Jane the picture without flipping it over to look at the back.

"You should look first," he told her.

"Thank you," Jane said and accepted the picture.

She turned it over in her palm and looked down at it. She was silent for a moment and then looked up at Simran.

"Success," she said.

"Did you find something out?" he asked.

Jane nodded.

"Success," she repeated. "That's what it says on the back of the picture. Just 'success', nothing else."

She handed the picture to Simran, who looked at it, flipped it over, read the word, and then flipped it over again. He handed it to Pyra.

"What do you think that means?" he asked.

"I don't know," Pyra answered, handing the picture over to Eden so that she could take her turn.

"What's strange about it," Jane said, "is that it was obviously taken quite a long time ago and it is using Earth technology and has Earth fashion, so I would venture to say that it was taken here. That doesn't make sense, though. You are the first Denynso to visit Earth."

"Except for Ero," Pyra said.

"Zuri's mate," Jane said and Simran nodded. "OK, yes, but he was here for one day and didn't go anywhere but from the university to get Zuri and back. Other than that, you are the first to come here. Human visits to Uoria only started about fifty years ago, and those humans were tourists. The exchange program and the visiting scientists and journalists are really the only possible means of interaction with the Denynso except for those early tourists who I doubt would have staged such a picture."

"That's not true," Eden said.

"You think that they would stage the picture?" Jane asked.

"No," Eden said. "That's not what I meant. You said that those tourists were the first opportunity that the humans had to interact with the Denynso. That there weren't any other means of interaction before that."

Simran sudden realized what Eden was talking about. He felt his heart pound slightly. He met Eden's eyes and they both turned to look at Pyra, who was already staring at them. He shook his head and gestured slightly toward Jane.

"What is it?" she asked. "What's going on?"

"Nothing," Simran said, heeding the nonverbal warning from his leader.

"Yes, there is," Jane replied. "There's something going on. What is it?"

"It isn't our story to tell, Simran," Eden warned.

"This is my mate, Eden," Simran said. "I have to tell her. I can't keep anything from her. Besides, she deserves to know as much as she can about her great-grandfather, even if we can only help her to figure out what this picture is all about."

"What is it?" Jane asked again.

Eden finally gave a nod of permission and Simran looked at Jane.

"What do you know about Nyx 23?" he asked.

There was a pause and Jane looked at him strangely as if she wasn't following what he was saying.

"Nyx 23," Eden repeated. "The mission team."

Jane continued to stare at him like she didn't know what

to think, and then her eyes widened. He could see recognition sinking in and her lips parted slightly before she spoke.

"The team that left here and never came back?" she asked. "I remember reading about it in school when I was younger, but I never knew the whole story."

"No one did," Eden said. "The official take was that they left here on a mission to free an illegal prison camp and were lost in transit. There was never any further communication from them and no signs of them were ever uncovered."

"Alright," Jane said. "What does that have to do with the Denynso?" she asked.

"We found them," Pyra said.

Jane's eyes snapped to him.

"What?" she asked sharply.

"We found them," Pyra repeated. "Well," he said, "we came upon them."

"It is a very long story," Eden said, "but for now suffice it to say that Nyx 23 was not lost. They weren't killed when they went to that planet and they didn't spiral out of orbit. They crash landed on Uoria and have been there ever since."

"Did they stay with the Denynso?" Jane asked.

"No," Pyra said. "They were on a different area of the planet. That still means, though, that there was more opportunity for interaction between the Denynso and the humans than we might have thought."

"Do you think that this picture was taken on Uoria?" Jane asked. "Maybe those are crew members of Nyx 23 and this picture was taken during an encounter with the Denynso?"

Pyra shook his head.

"I don't think so," he said. "They don't look familiar."

"What do you mean?" Jane asked.

"Is there someone who we can ask?" Eden asked,

seeming to want to brush the question away. "Maybe someone who is a bit more familiar with what the team looked like?"

Simran nodded.

"I'll be right back,"

He took the picture and rushed down the stairs into the living room where Brandy sat. He crouched down beside her and held the picture so that she could see it.

"Were any of those men on the crew?" he asked.

Brandy looked slightly startled, but took the picture and held it carefully as she examined it.

"Where did you get this picture?" she asked.

"That doesn't matter right now. We're trying to figure out what it is. Do you recognize any of those men?"

She looked at it again and shook her head.

"None of them was on the crew," she said. "This one, though," she said with a slight laugh as she pointed to the man standing closest to the Denynso in the picture, "he looks like Captain Francisco."

"Captain Francisco?" Simran asked.

"Yeah. He was part of a military operative who we sometimes worked with. He was a good thirty years younger than this man, though."

She handed him back the picture and Simran took it, his fingers closing slowly around it as he let her words sink in.

TBC

(To be continued in book VIII...)